DISNEY'S
THE
HUNCHBACK
OF NOTRE DAME

A catalogue record for this book is available from the British Library

Published by Ladybird Books Ltd
A subsidiary of the Penguin Group
A Pearson Company
LADYBIRD and the device of a Ladybird are trademarks of Ladybird Books Ltd Loughborough Leicestershire UK

Disney's

THE HUNCHBACK OF NOTRE DAME

Ladybird

I

As the sun rose over Paris, it warmed the cobblestone streets and the river that flows through the city. It shone on gabled rooftops and the spires of the towering cathedral. By mid-morning, the slanting rays brightened the chilly bell tower. There, the faithful bell ringer was at work. As he tugged at the thick ropes, the huge bells rang out, sounding the hour. They were the bells of the great cathedral of Notre Dame.

Below, in the town square, children gathered to watch a puppet show. "Listen to them, my little ones," said the puppeteer, "the bells—they are beautiful, no? But do you know who is ringing them? Do you know that high in the tower of Notre Dame lives a mysterious bell ringer?"

The puppeteer removed his feathered hat with a sweeping bow.

"I, Clopin, the leader of the gypsies," he announced, "will tell you a tale about this man. And I can tell you it is true because I have witnessed much of it with my own eyes—and heard of it with my own ears!"

He drew in a deep breath and began his story.

"It is the tale of a man and a monster. Listen carefully, my children," Clopin told them, "then maybe you can tell me—who is the man... and who is the monster?"

II

One winter's night the city lay dusted in fresh snow. While the citizens slept, a small boat glided down the river past the cathedral. A group of wary travellers huddled on board and peered anxiously into the dark. As the boat docked beside an ice-coated pier, the only sounds were the splashing of the oars and a baby's whimper. "Keep the child still," a nervous passenger warned. "You know we gypsies are not welcome here in Paris."

The infant's mother gently hugged her son. "Hush, little one," she whispered. But the mother's words came too late.

Armed soldiers sprang from the shadows and surrounded the gypsies as they stepped ashore. A black stallion, its breath frosting in the moonlight, stood silently nearby.

One of the gypsies gasped. He recognised the horse's rider – "Judge Claude Frollo!" he gulped. He knew that this man, the Minister of Justice, had a reputation for cruelty.

"Take the gypsies to the Palace of Justice," Frollo ordered.

One soldier noticed the bundled baby. "You there!" he cried, stopping the child's mother. "What are you hiding?"

"Stolen goods, no doubt," said Frollo. "Seize them."

The soldier tried to snatch the blanket but the woman fled into the night holding her precious baby tightly in her arms. Frollo spurred his horse and began to pursue her.

With the sound of the stallion's pounding hoofbeats ringing in her ears, the terrified woman tried desperately to run across the slippery, ice-covered streets. *If I can just reach the cathedral,* she thought, *my baby and I will be safe. Once inside, we will be granted sanctuary – the sacred protection of the Church.*

At the end of an alleyway, a narrow gate blocked her way. The woman frantically fumbled with the latch, and as Frollo rode hard towards her, she squeezed through. Furious, Frollo directed his horse to a wider passage.

The woman scrambled up the wide stone steps of Notre Dame and pounded on the heavy arched doors.

"Sanctuary!" she cried. "Please, give us sanctuary!"

Frollo, spurring his galloping stallion, thundered up behind her. He leaned down and tugged at the tightly clutched bundle. Knocked off balance, the gypsy woman lost her footing and hit her head against a step. Frollo coldly viewed her still body and knew she would never rise again.

Suddenly, the baby began to wail.

"An infant?" Frollo uttered in surprise. He peered inside the blanket. He could see at a glance that the child was misshapen. "A monster!" the Minister of Justice declared. Frollo guided his horse towards a stone well at the edge of the courtyard. His eyes gleamed as he dangled the wriggling bundle above the dark opening. "I will send this unholy demon back to hell..." he began.

"*Stop!*" demanded a voice.

Frollo spun around. A robed man wearing a priest's cowl looked up at him, angrily.

"Archdeacon!" gasped Frollo.

"You have killed an innocent creature of God," said the churchman.

"She ran — I merely pursued her," Frollo protested.

The Archdeacon shook his head. "It is because of you she is dead," he said. "And now you would kill her unfortunate infant, too."

"My conscience is clear," insisted Frollo.

"You have sinned," declared the Archdeacon. "If you wish to save your soul, you must make up for your wickedness by caring for this child as you would your own."

Frollo's face flushed with rage. But he also feared for his immortal soul.

The Archdeacon pointed to the statues of saints gazing sternly from the heights of the cathedral. Frollo stared up at the statue of Notre Dame, 'Our Lady', protecting her own infant in her arms.

Frollo weighed the consequences of his decision. *Actually, he thought, if I keep the child locked up in the tower, the situation just might be tolerable. One day, the child could even prove useful to me.*

"Very well, Archdeacon," he said, forcing a thin smile. "I'll provide for the child and teach him what he needs to know. But let him live here with you, within the cathedral."

"Very well," the Archdeacon agreed.

Frollo glared at the tiny baby. *It is almost ironic,* he thought to himself. *This monstrous child will be kept in the bell tower with only the gargoyles for companions. Now those hideous stone creatures will have a rival in ugliness!*

And because Frollo thought the child was more monster than human, he named him Quasimodo, which means 'the Half-Formed One'.

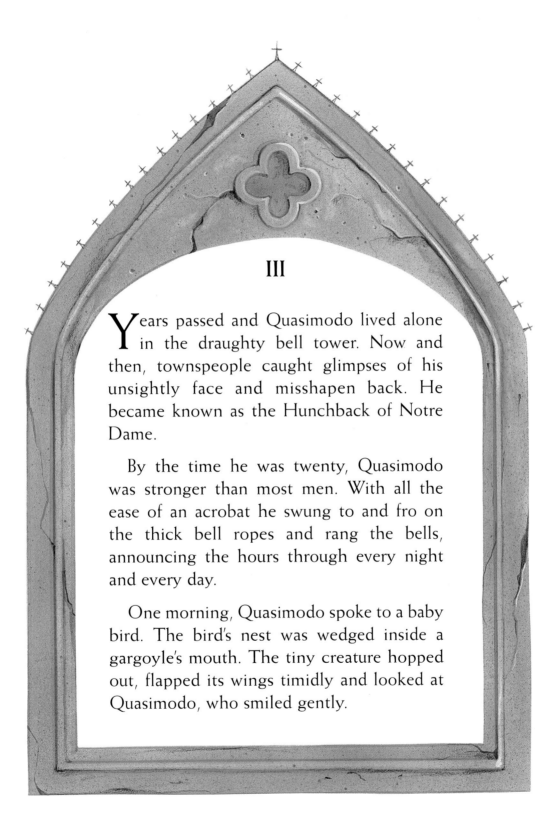

III

Years passed and Quasimodo lived alone in the draughty bell tower. Now and then, townspeople caught glimpses of his unsightly face and misshapen back. He became known as the Hunchback of Notre Dame.

By the time he was twenty, Quasimodo was stronger than most men. With all the ease of an acrobat he swung to and fro on the thick bell ropes and rang the bells, announcing the hours through every night and every day.

One morning, Quasimodo spoke to a baby bird. The bird's nest was wedged inside a gargoyle's mouth. The tiny creature hopped out, flapped its wings timidly and looked at Quasimodo, who smiled gently.

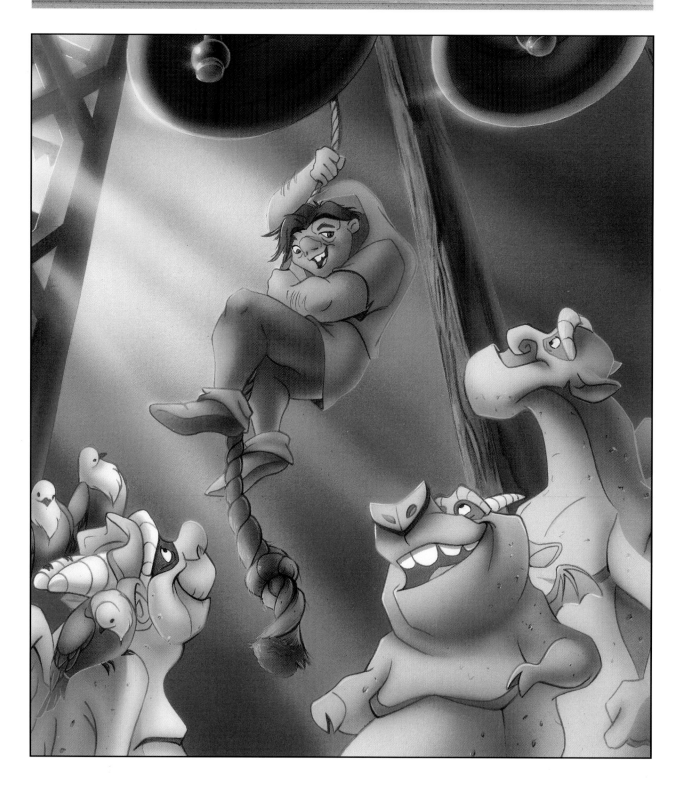

"Go on," Quasimodo encouraged the little bird. "Nobody wants to be cooped up here forever. Why, if I picked a day to fly, this would be it—the Festival of Fools! It will be fun down there in the square. You'll see jugglers and dancing, and eat wonderful food!"

The bird began to flap its wings a little more enthusiastically, until suddenly, it took off. As soon as it had flown away, the gargoyle came to life.

"*Pleccch!* I thought that little guy'd never leave," he said as he coughed and spat the bird's nest out of his mouth. "I'll be spittin' out feathers for a week."

Nearby, another gargoyle spoke up. "That's what you get for sleeping with your mouth open, Hugo," he said primly. He stretched and extended his wings.

"Ah, Victor, go get lost," Hugo replied.

The gargoyles leaned over the rail and watched the noisy crowds.

"This is a great spot," said Hugo. "Balcony seats!"

"It is such a treat to watch the colourful pageantry of the simple peasant folk," Victor observed. "Although it is *such* a peculiar celebration—imagine dressing up as foolishly as possible. And then, as the grand finale, the most foolish-looking of them all is crowned the king of the festival!"

"Don't be so stuffy, Victor," said Hugo. "Listen, the band's tuning up." He leaned over the rail. "Quick, Quasi, the tightrope walker's putting up his rope!" He glanced around. "Quasi? Hey! Where're you goin'?"

"Don't you want to watch the festival with us?" asked Victor. "Are you ill?"

"Impossible," cackled an elderly gargoyle, as she shuffled towards them. "If twenty years of listening to you two hasn't made him ill, nothing will!"

"But, Laverne," Victor told her, "watching the Festival of Fools has always been the highlight of the year for Quasimodo."

"He's right," said Hugo. "Let's go find out what's the matter."

They found Quasimodo at a table, gazing at a miniature wooden town. He'd carved it himself. It was a model of the city he knew only from high above in the bell tower.

"What's wrong, Quasi?" asked Laverne. "Wanna tell Laverne all about it?"

"I... I just don't feel like watching the festival, that's all," said Quasimodo.

Laverne scratched her chin for a moment. "Did you ever think of *going* there instead?" she asked.

"Good idea," agreed Victor. "As your friends and guardians, we insist that you attend the festival!"

"Yeah," said Hugo. "Quit beatin' around the bell tower."

"But I'd never fit in out there. I'm not... normal," said Quasimodo, sadly.

"Quasi, Quasi," Laverne said, gently, "take it from an old spectator. Life's not a spectator sport. If watching is all you're gonna do, then you're gonna watch your life go by without you."

"I appreciate all the encouragement," interrupted Quasimodo, "but you're forgetting one big thing – my master, Frollo."

"Ooh," said Laverne. "I did forget for a minute."

"Tell me," said Victor, "when Frollo says you're forbidden to ever leave the bell tower, does he mean ever… ever?"

"He means *never* ever!" said Quasimodo. "And he hates the Festival of Fools. He'd be furious if I even *asked* to go."

"Well then," said Hugo, wiggling his eyebrows, "who says you gotta *ask?*"

"It's just one afternoon," urged Laverne.

"Sure," said Hugo. "You sneak out… and sneak back in."

"But he might see me," said Quasimodo.

"You could wear a disguise," suggested Victor.

"Remember what you told that little bird," Laverne reminded him. "'Nobody wants to stay cooped up here forever'."

Quasimodo thought it over for a moment. "You're right," he declared. "I'll go!"

"That's the stuff!" yelled Hugo.

Victor patted Quasimodo on the back. "You'll see," he said, "this decision is one you'll not regret."

Beaming from ear to ear, Laverne opened the door wide. Then all at once she froze. Frollo himself was coming up the stairs!

"Oh! G-g-good morning, Master," stammered Quasimodo, fearfully.

"Dear boy, whoever were you talking to?" asked Frollo.

Quasimodo hesitated for a moment. "My friends," he answered.

"I see," said Frollo, knocking his hand against Laverne's suddenly still forehead. "And what are your friends made of?"

"Stone," answered Quasimodo.

"Can stone talk?" asked Frollo.

"No, Master," answered Quasimodo.

"Smart lad!" said Frollo. "Well then, let's sit down. First, we shall review your alphabet. *A* is for?..."

"Abomination," recited Quasimodo.

Frollo nodded. "*B*?..."

"Is for blasphemy," Quasimodo responded. "*C* is for contrition. *D* is for damnation. *E* is for eternal damnation. *F* is for festival..."

"Excuse me?" interrupted Frollo.

"I mean, f-f-forgiveness!"

"You said 'festival'," roared Frollo. "You are thinking about going to the Festival of Fools!"

"It's just that... you get to go every year, and..." Quasimodo faltered.

"I am a public official," Frollo interrupted. "I *must* go. But I don't enjoy it. Thieves and pickpockets—the dregs of humankind, all mixed together in a shallow, crazy stupor." He shook his head with mock sadness. "When your heartless mother abandoned you, no one but I took you in. Is this the thanks you give me for rearing you as a son?"

Quasimodo looked ashamed. "You've been good to me, Master," he said, miserably. "I didn't mean to upset you."

"You are forgiven," said Frollo, pausing at the door. He patted Quasimodo on the shoulder. "You don't know what it's like out there. *I* do. The world is a cruel place. You would be hated and scorned. Only this place can be a sanctuary to one such as you." And with that, Frollo swept from the room.

Alone, Quasimodo went back to his miniature town. He took a tiny carved model from inside the little bell tower. It was of himself. He placed it in the middle of the town square.

"All my life," he said, softly, "I've wanted to be there. If only for a day." Quasimodo went out onto the balcony and longingly watched the happy crowds below. *If I were down there*, he thought, *I'd love every minute—going where I wished, stopping where I might...*

He raised his face to heaven and closed his eyes. "Oh, if I could have but one day of freedom to hold forever in my heart..." he murmured.

In a few moments, Quasimodo opened his eyes. Then, with a new, determined air, he went back to his room and threw on his cloak. He would be going to the festival after all!

IV

Aman led his horse through the crowded festival streets. The man's name was Phoebus. Hidden beneath his cloak, he wore the golden armour of a captain in the Royal Army. Puzzled, he stopped to check his crumpled map. "It should be around here somewhere, Achilles," Phoebus muttered to his horse. "Perhaps we took a wrong turn." Achilles whinnied and sidestepped around a man playing a flute. Close by was a white goat with a gold ring in his ear. A delighted crowd threw coins onto the street as the animal danced and a gypsy girl waved a tambourine.

Phoebus stopped to watch and threw a few coins. The gypsy girl looked up at him and smiled. Phoebus smiled back—he'd never seen anyone so beautiful!

Suddenly, another gypsy at the edge of the crowd whistled a shrill warning.

"Esmeralda!" he cried. "The money!"

Esmeralda fell to her knees, scooping the stray coins into a hat. As she found the last one, two soldiers pushed their way through the crowd. The shorter of the two wore a lieutenant's stripes. The other was a sergeant with a bushy moustache. They pulled Esmeralda to her feet.

"All right, where did you get the money?" demanded the lieutenant. He snatched the hat from her grasp.

"I earned it," protested Esmeralda. "Give it back!"

He held the hat above her head. "Gypsies don't earn money. They steal it," his comrade proclaimed.

Esmeralda reached up for the hat. The lieutenant raised it higher. She kicked him hard in the shin and he yelped with pain.

The sergeant grabbed Esmeralda by the wrist. "Maybe a few days in prison will cool you down," he said.

"Djali!" shouted Esmeralda. Springing into action, the little goat scrambled through everybody's legs and butted the soldier. As the man lost his balance, Esmeralda broke free. She and Djali darted past Phoebus.

Phoebus raised his eyebrows. *Very impressive*, he thought. *Very impressive, indeed.*

The furious soldiers charged forward. Phoebus pulled hard on Achilles' reins and blocked their way.

"Achilles, sit!" he ordered.

At once, the obedient animal sat down – on the sergeant.

"Hey! Get this thing off me!" the sergeant cried out.

"Oh my. I *am* sorry!" said Phoebus with mock concern. "This horse is impossible – he can't be taken anywhere."

Esmeralda, watching from a safe distance, grinned. Then she and Djali vanished into the crowd.

The lieutenant drew a dagger. "I'll teach you a lesson… peasant!"

As Phoebus flung back his cloak to draw his sword, his armour was revealed. Recognising Phoebus' rank, the soldier snapped to attention.

"At your s-service, Captain," he stammered.

Phoebus pulled up on the reins. As Achilles stood up, the sergeant scrambled out from underneath the horse. Glaring, he jumped to his feet and reluctantly saluted.

"And now, you two," Phoebus said, "I wish to be escorted to the Palace of Justice."

V

The immense Palace of Justice faced an open square packed with festival-goers. Phoebus stepped from the sunny day into the building's gloomy halls. "I am looking for Judge Frollo," he told an approaching guard.

"Down in the dungeon," the guard answered, gesturing to a stairwell. "He's overseeing the punishment of a prisoner."

Phoebus made his way down the winding stone steps. Torchlight flickered on the damp walls and fat water bugs scurried past his feet. Every now and then the crack of a whip cut the dark silence. The awful sound grew louder as he descended the stairs into the darkness.

Frollo, standing at the open cell door near the foot of the stairs, greeted Phoebus.

"Ah, so *you* are the gallant Captain Phoebus, home from the wars," he said.

"Reporting for duty as ordered, Sir," answered Phoebus. "I'm looking forward to working under your command."

"Your record as a war hero precedes you," said Frollo. "I have no doubt that you will be a vast improvement over the man who formerly served under me. He proved most unsatisfactory." Frollo gestured towards the cell. "I am finished with my work here for the moment. Come, I wish to show you something from up on the colonnade," he said.

Phoebus followed Frollo back up the steps and onto a wide balcony lined with columns.

"Tell me what you see," said Frollo, pointing to the noisy festival crowd below.

Phoebus leaned against the colonnade railing and gazed across the sunny square.

"People just having a good time?" he asked.

"*Misled, confused* people," Frollo corrected him. "You've come to Paris in her darkest hour, Captain. It will take a firm hand such as yours to save our many weak-minded citizens."

"From what?" asked Phoebus.

"From the gypsies," Frollo told him.

Phoebus was surprised. "Gypsies? What have they done?"

"They are a bad influence on our people," Frollo explained. "They do whatever they please, go wherever they like." His eyes narrowed and his voice grew harsh. "For twenty years I have fought to keep them under control. Yet, despite all my efforts, they have thrived."

Frollo then noticed a line of tiny ants along the stone railing. They marched past his hand and disappeared beneath a crack. He lifted the loose piece of railing. Hundreds of disturbed insects swarmed out from their hidden nest.

Looking at the ants, he continued. "I believe the gypsies have a safe haven within the very walls of this city – a nest, if you will." He sneered. "They refer to it as the Court of Miracles."

"What are we going to do about it, Sir?" asked Phoebus.

Frollo smashed the brick down, crushing the ants and their nest.

"I see," said Phoebus. "You've made yourself clear."

Frollo smiled. "Now let's go and see what those peasants are up to."

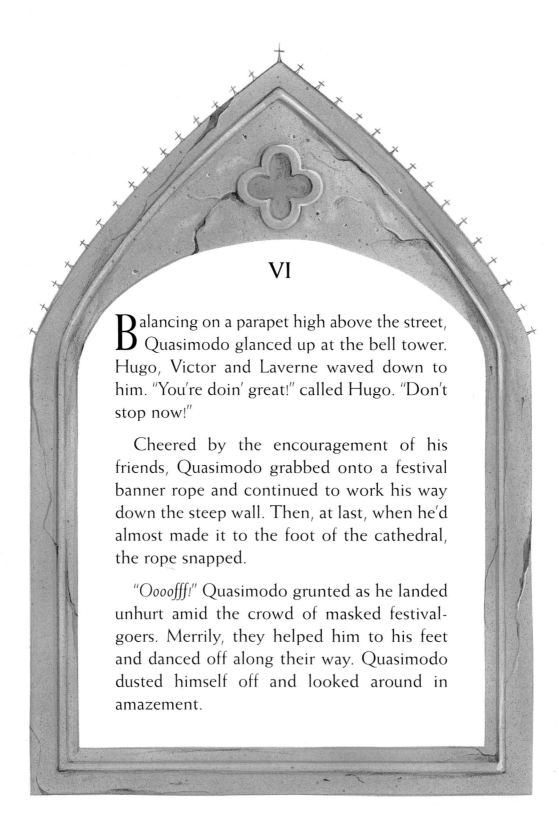

VI

Balancing on a parapet high above the street, Quasimodo glanced up at the bell tower. Hugo, Victor and Laverne waved down to him. "You're doin' great!" called Hugo. "Don't stop now!"

Cheered by the encouragement of his friends, Quasimodo grabbed onto a festival banner rope and continued to work his way down the steep wall. Then, at last, when he'd almost made it to the foot of the cathedral, the rope snapped.

"*Oooofff!*" Quasimodo grunted as he landed unhurt amid the crowd of masked festival-goers. Merrily, they helped him to his feet and danced off along their way. Quasimodo dusted himself off and looked around in amazement.

The mobbed streets were a little scary. Taking a deep breath, Quasimodo joined the jostling crowd.

Enticing aromas hung in the air, and the lively, raucous sounds of horns and drums vibrated in his head.

People were dressed in an amazing array of funny, topsy turvy costumes. A man in a dog outfit strolled by, walking a man on a lead. Then two people dressed as a horse with a tail at both ends bumped into him. Regaining his balance, Quasimodo was almost knocked over again by a man on stilts.

Confused and disorientated, Quasimodo desperately tried to find somewhere to shelter from the commotion. He stumbled into a dressing tent next to a wooden stage and bumped against a table, knocking everything on it to the ground.

Esmeralda, who was brushing her hair, rushed towards him.

"Are you all right?" she asked.

"I'm sorry," said Quasimodo. "I didn't mean to…"

Esmeralda helped him to his feet. "No harm done," she said. She showed him the way out of the tent. "Why don't you stay and watch the show?"

"Th-thank you," stammered Quasimodo. "That would be very nice."

"By the way," said Esmeralda, grinning at him, "great mask!"

Quasimodo turned away, shy and embarrassed. Then he left Esmeralda's tent and hesitantly joined the crowd outside.

"Come one, come all – see the lovely Esmeralda dance!" a man shouted to the crowd. "I, Clopin, the leader of the gypsies, welcome you!" He threw some powder into the air and it exploded into a puff

of coloured smoke. When the air cleared, Esmeralda stood before the cheering crowd.

As she began to dance and play her tambourine, Quasimodo's heart thumped wildly – he could never have imagined anyone so beautiful.

Seated near the stage and frowning, Frollo watched Esmeralda dance. She glided over to him and playfully tipped his hat forward. Frollo moved away. But he could see that his companion, Phoebus, was clearly enchanted by her.

As she returned to the stage to finish her dance, Esmeralda winked at Quasimodo. Half hidden in his hood, he blushed and lowered his eyes.

Clopin stepped forward and raised his hands to quieten the applauding crowd. "And now the moment you've all been waiting for," he announced. "It's time to crown the king of this year's Festival of Fools. Because our festival's a time when everything's topsy turvy, the King of the Fools must have the ugliest face in town."

Clopin faced the crowd. "Contestants, take your places," he cried. "Take a good look at them all. As Esmeralda removes the masks, vote with your applause for the one which is the most frightening and horrible!"

Esmeralda went straight over to Quasimodo. "Come on," she whispered to him. "Come up on stage with the others. You're sure to win!"

"No, no," he protested. "Please..."

Refusing to give up, Esmeralda pulled him by the hand. He had no choice but to go. As he stepped up to the stage, Quasimodo's cloak slipped from his back.

The other contestants climbed up and stood next to him. A man wearing a fish head paraded past. Others sported heads of serpents, sharp-beaked birds and sea monsters. One contestant wore the face of a gargoyle.

Esmeralda began to remove the masks. The crowd cheered or booed for each of them.

"Now *here's* a really ugly mask," Clopin said when Esmeralda reached Quasimodo. "Esmeralda, take off this man's mask so we can see who he is."

Esmeralda gently tugged at Quasimodo's face. "Oh!" she exclaimed, realising it wasn't a mask.

Quasimodo frantically looked for an escape. But the stage whirled before his eyes and he felt faint.

"It's Quasimodo," someone cried. "It's the bell ringer from the cathedral."

Ashamed and frightened, Quasimodo buried his face in his hands.

"Ladies and gentlemen," announced Clopin, "we asked for the ugliest face in all of Paris, and here it is – Quasimodo, the Hunchback of Notre Dame!"

"Quasimodo! Quasimodo!" roared the crowd, rushing forward enthusiastically, as Clopin crowned him the King of Fools.

Lifting him high on their shoulders, the crowd paraded out into the street. Quasimodo felt an unexpected surge of happiness. Frollo had been wrong. The people didn't hate him at all – he was going to be their king!

But then the lieutenant who'd chased Esmeralda that morning

yelled to the crowd, "You think he's ugly now — watch this!" Taking aim, he threw a juicy tomato at Quasimodo.

It hit Quasimodo square on the head. Other people joined in, pelting him with fruit.

"Gifts from your loyal subjects!" the lieutenant jeered.

"Stop it!" shouted Esmeralda. But her voice was lost in the uproar.

Someone threw a rope around Quasimodo and tied him to a pillory wheel. Laughing, the crowd threw more fruit at him. Straining at the ropes, Quasimodo looked about wildly for help. He spotted Frollo and a tall soldier watching nearby.

"Master!" he cried out to Frollo. "Master, please help me!"

Frollo sat still.

"Sir," said Phoebus, sitting beside him. "I request your permission to put a stop to this cruelty." He put his hand to his sword hilt and got ready to stand up.

"In a moment," replied Frollo, coolly, a smile playing about his lips. "A lesson needs to be learnt here."

Esmeralda made her way towards the pillory. Quasimodo, frightened and embarrassed, leaned away from her.

"Don't be afraid," she whispered. She began to wipe Quasimodo's face with her scarf. The rowdy crowd suddenly grew quiet and watched.

"Stop that at once!" Frollo ordered Esmeralda. "At *once!*"

"Yes, Your Honour," answered Esmeralda. "Just as soon as I free this poor creature."

Frollo was enraged. "I forbid it!"

Esmeralda cut Quasimodo's rope.

"How dare you defy me!" Frollo roared.

"You mistreat this poor boy the same way you mistreat my people," Esmeralda protested. "You're the Minister of Justice—but cruellest to those who need your help the most!"

"Silence!" Frollo shouted.

"Justice!" Esmeralda shouted back.

The crowd gasped, astonished at her boldness.

"Mark my words," said Frollo through clenched teeth, "you will pay for this insolence."

"Then it appears," Esmeralda told him, removing Quasimodo's crown, "that we've crowned the wrong fool today. The only fool I see is… you!"

She threw the crown at Frollo's feet. Delighted, the crowd cheered.

Frollo signalled to Phoebus. "Arrest her!"

Esmeralda laughed. "Just try it!" she challenged him. She threw some powder into the air and, hidden behind a puff of smoke, ran off with Djali at her heels. The soldiers followed, but before they could reach her she had disappeared, dodging and weaving her way through the crowd.

"This gypsy's defiance and trickery must stop, Captain," Frollo said to Phoebus. "Find her and bring her to me!" Then he glared at Quasimodo.

"I'm sorry, Master," said Quasimodo. Tears streamed down his cheeks. "I will never disobey you again."

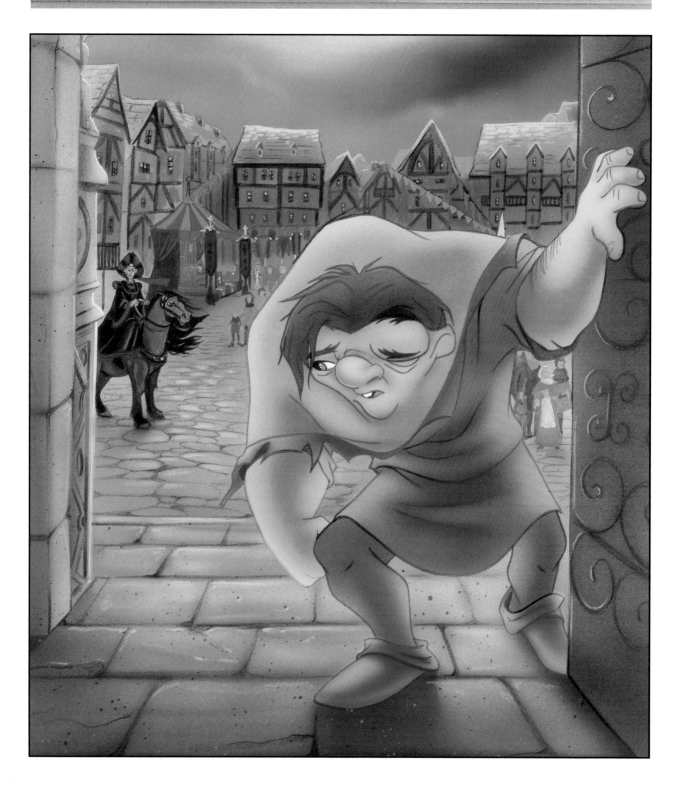

From the parapet, the gargoyles looked on sadly as their friend, his head hung in shame, trudged up the steps to the cathedral. Quasimodo knew he would never again leave Notre Dame against Frollo's wishes.

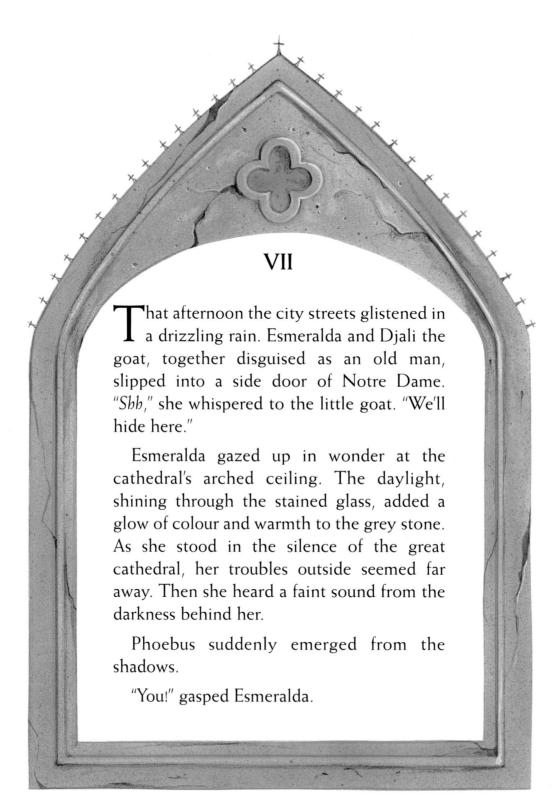

VII

That afternoon the city streets glistened in a drizzling rain. Esmeralda and Djali the goat, together disguised as an old man, slipped into a side door of Notre Dame. "*Shh*," she whispered to the little goat. "We'll hide here."

Esmeralda gazed up in wonder at the cathedral's arched ceiling. The daylight, shining through the stained glass, added a glow of colour and warmth to the grey stone. As she stood in the silence of the great cathedral, her troubles outside seemed far away. Then she heard a faint sound from the darkness behind her.

Phoebus suddenly emerged from the shadows.

"You!" gasped Esmeralda.

Phoebus nodded. "You gave us quite a chase."

Esmeralda grabbed a candelabra and held it in the air. "Don't come any closer," she warned him.

Phoebus smiled. "I was just coming to apologise." He bowed. "My name is Phoebus." He paused and grinned. "It means 'Sun God'."

Esmeralda grinned back. Then she grew serious. "You're not arresting me?"

"Not as long as you're in here," said Phoebus. "You have sanctuary. You can't be arrested if you ask for the protection of the Church."

Esmeralda was confused. "If you're not going to arrest me, then what do you want?"

Phoebus smiled. "I'd settle for an introduction."

Esmeralda hesitated for a few seconds, then told him her name.

"Esmeralda," repeated Phoebus, softly. "It's a beautiful name."

The sound of footsteps made them turn. Frollo, escorted by two soldiers, approached them. "Good work, Captain," he said, smiling broadly. "Now arrest the gypsy."

"You tricked me," she said, sounding both disappointed and furious.

Phoebus drew his sword and approached Esmeralda. "Claim sanctuary," he whispered to her.

Frollo spoke. "I'm waiting, Captain."

Phoebus turned to him. "I'm sorry, Sir," he reported, "but she has claimed sanctuary. There's nothing I can do."

Esmeralda trembled with relief — the soldier had saved her!

"Well then, drag her outside," said Frollo. "You can arrest her there. Then take her to…"

An angry voice interrupted him. "You will not touch her!" The Archdeacon, his robe billowing behind him, crossed the stone floor. He motioned with a sweeping gesture to Frollo. "You must leave Notre Dame."

He turned to Esmeralda. "Do not be frightened. Minister Frollo learnt years ago to respect the sanctity of the Church. You've been granted sanctuary – so long as you remain here, you are safe."

As the Archdeacon ushered the soldiers out, Frollo leaned close to Esmeralda's ear. "You think you've outwitted me," he hissed. "But I am a patient man. And we both know gypsies don't do well inside stone walls. You've chosen a magnificent place to stay. But it's a prison nonetheless. Set one foot outside Notre Dame and you're mine!"

As soon as he left, Esmeralda ran to the door. With Djali at her side, she peered out. A soldier stood at every exit. "Don't worry," she said to the little goat. "If Frollo thinks he can keep us here, he's wrong!"

The Archdeacon came up behind her. "Don't act rashly, my child," he warned her. "It would be unwise to rouse Frollo's anger any further."

"I thought if just one person could stand up to him, then…"

The Archdeacon smiled, sadly. "You can't right all the wrongs of this world by yourself."

"Well, one thing is for sure," said Esmeralda, "no one out there is going to help."

"Perhaps," suggested the Archdeacon, looking towards the altar, "there is someone in here who can."

He left her alone. In the silence of Notre Dame, Esmeralda closed her eyes and prayed. When she raised her head, she saw Quasimodo watching her. As soon as their eyes met, he ran for the door leading to the bell tower.

"Wait!" Esmeralda called out, running after him. "I'd like to talk to you."

VIII

Quasimodo charged up the steps into the bell tower. "Got the girls chasin' you already?" Hugo teased.

"You mustn't run too fast," advised Victor, "or she'll get away!"

Hugo began casting an imaginary fishing line. "You gotta give her some slack, then reel 'er in," he said. "Then give 'er some slack, then reel 'er in. Then—*ow!*" he grunted as Laverne bopped him on the head.

"Knock it off, Hugo!" Laverne told him. "She's a woman, not a mackerel!"

"Hush, you two," warned Victor. "There's someone coming."

Esmeralda, with Djali at her heels, burst into the room. "Here you are," she cried.

Esmeralda stopped to catch her breath. "I was afraid I'd lost you," she said.

"Yes… well, I have… things to do… it was nice… seeing you… again…" mumbled Quasimodo. He started for an open door. "Er, I gotta go now."

"Wait," Esmeralda said. "I'm really sorry about what happened this afternoon." She glanced about the room and noticed the miniature town on the table.

"Did you make that all by yourself?" she asked, going over for a closer look.

Quasimodo nodded.

Esmeralda looked at the little buildings with gabled rooftops and the tiny townspeople. In the centre of the city stood a perfectly carved model of Notre Dame.

"This is beautiful," said Esmeralda. "If I had your talent, you wouldn't find me dancing in the streets for coins."

"But you're a wonderful dancer," said Quasimodo.

"Well, it keeps bread on the table," said Esmeralda with a shrug. She spotted two little carved figures sticking out beneath a cloth.

"Oh no," Quasimodo protested. "Please… they're not finished. They're not even painted yet."

But Esmeralda was already looking at them. "It's the blacksmith," she laughed, "and the baker!"

"Yes," said Quasimodo. "I hope to carve all the townspeople one day."

Esmeralda studied the perfect little carvings.

"You're a surprising person, Quasimodo," she said. She looked around her. "And a lucky one—having this whole tower to yourself."

"It's not just me," Quasimodo explained. "There's the gargoyles. And of course the bells—would you like to see them?"

Esmeralda followed him up a narrow ladder. Djali nimbly climbed up behind her.

"Look at all these bells," said Esmeralda, stepping onto the platform. "I never knew there were so many."

"Each one has a name," Quasimodo told her, pointing them out. "That one is Little Sophie. And these are Jeanne-Marie, Anne-Marie and Louise-Marie… they're triplets."

Esmeralda laughed. Then she looked up into an enormous bell hanging above her head. "And who's this?"

"Big Marie!" answered Quasimodo.

Quasimodo gently took Esmeralda by the arm and pointed out an arched window. "I saved the best for last. We can see even better from outside," said Quasimodo.

"*Outside?*"

"There's a little stairway leading to the roof," he said. "Just be careful up there!"

It was now sunset. All over the city people were lighting lamps in their houses. As they watched, the river turned from rose to dark blue. Then the stars began to twinkle in the black night sky.

"I bet the king himself doesn't have a view like this," said Esmeralda. "I could stay up here forever."

"Well, you could, you know," Quasimodo told her. "You have sanctuary."

Esmeralda shook her head. "Sanctuary, but not freedom. We gypsies don't do well inside stone walls. Even Frollo understands that."

"But you aren't like other gypsies," Quasimodo said. "They're... evil."

"Who told you that?" asked Esmeralda.

"My master, Frollo," said Quasimodo, proudly. "He raised me."

Esmeralda was surprised. "*He* raised *you?* But he's so cruel!"

"Cruel? Oh no, he saved my life," explained Quasimodo. "He took me in when no one else would. I'm a monster, you know."

"He told you that?" asked Esmeralda.

Quasimodo nodded.

Esmeralda gently took his hand. "Let me see." She studied the lines on his palm. "These lines say a lot about people, you know. Hmmmm. This one means you're shy... and intelligent, too."

"Really?" asked Quasimodo.

"That's funny," continued Esmeralda. "I don't see any..."

Quasimodo peered closer. "Any what?"

"Monster lines." Esmeralda showed him his hand. "Not a single one," she said. "Now, look at me, Quasimodo. Do you think I'm evil?"

"Oh no!" answered Quasimodo. "You're kind and good and..."

"And a *gypsy*," said Esmeralda. "So you see, maybe Frollo is wrong about both of us."

Quasimodo looked down and watched the soldiers parade back and forth in front of the cathedral.

"You helped me. Now I would like to help you," he told her.

"But there's no way to escape," said Esmeralda. "Frollo has soldiers posted at every door."

Quasimodo smiled, slyly. "We won't use a door."

Esmeralda swallowed hard. "You mean… *climb* down?"

"Sure," said Quasimodo. "That's how I got to the festival. Just pick up your goat. It'll be easy." Quasimodo got to his feet. "You carry him. And I'll carry you. Ready?" he asked.

"Well," said Esmeralda, "I'm not sure."

Quasimodo carefully picked her up. "Don't be afraid."

"I'm not afraid," Esmeralda said, firmly.

"Here we go!" Quasimodo took a wide leap over the ledge and grabbed the parapet. Together they dangled high over the city. Djali let out a loud bleat.

"*Now* I'm afraid!" said Esmeralda.

Quasimodo shifted his weight a bit. "The trick is not to look down."

"You've done this before?" asked Esmeralda, as Quasimodo leapt across the front of the cathedral.

"Er, not exactly," Quasimodo admitted.

Esmeralda gulped, closed her eyes and held on tightly.

Quasimodo landed lightly on a huge support that arched out from the side of the cathedral.

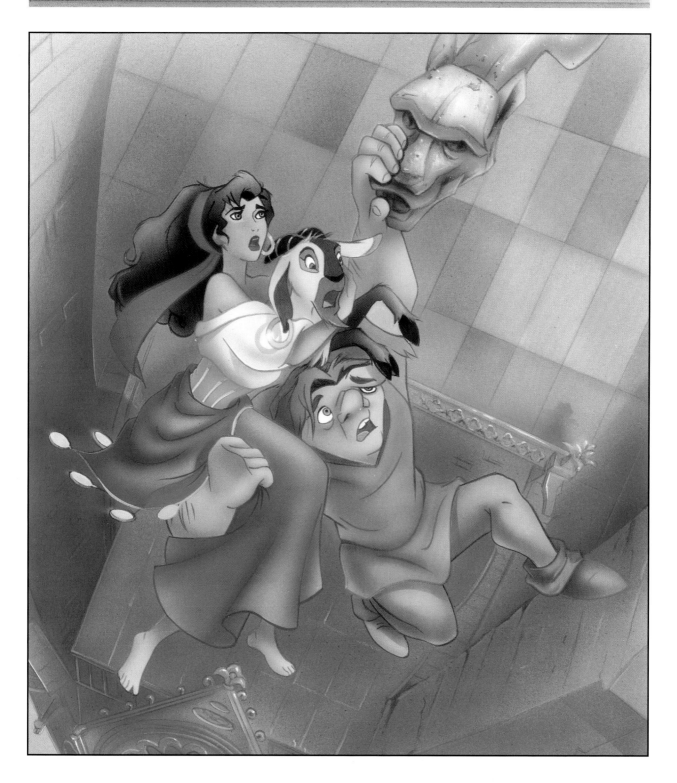

Esmeralda was impressed. "Say, you're really good at this," she said.

Suddenly, a tile broke loose under his foot and Quasimodo slipped. "Hold on!" he yelled.

They slid all the way down, stopping a short distance from the edge.

"Made it!" Quasimodo said, proudly.

A dislodged stone shot out into the air and tumbled to the street. Two passing soldiers looked up. Then they shrugged their shoulders and walked on.

"They didn't see us," whispered Esmeralda.

"It's only a little way to the ground—you can easily jump. I hope you weren't too scared," said Quasimodo.

"Not at all—not for an instant!" joked Esmeralda.

Quasimodo smiled. "I'll never forget you, Esmeralda."

Esmeralda gently touched his face. "Come with me."

"What?" Quasimodo couldn't believe his ears.

"Right now!" Esmeralda's eyes shone brightly. "Leave this place."

"Oh, but Frollo would be so upset," said Quasimodo. "No. No… this is where I belong."

Esmeralda could see he'd made up his mind. "All right then. I'll come to see you."

"Here?" asked Quasimodo, surprised. "What about the soldiers—and Frollo?"

"I'll sneak in after sunset!" Esmeralda said. She kissed him on the cheek, and Quasimodo blushed bright red.

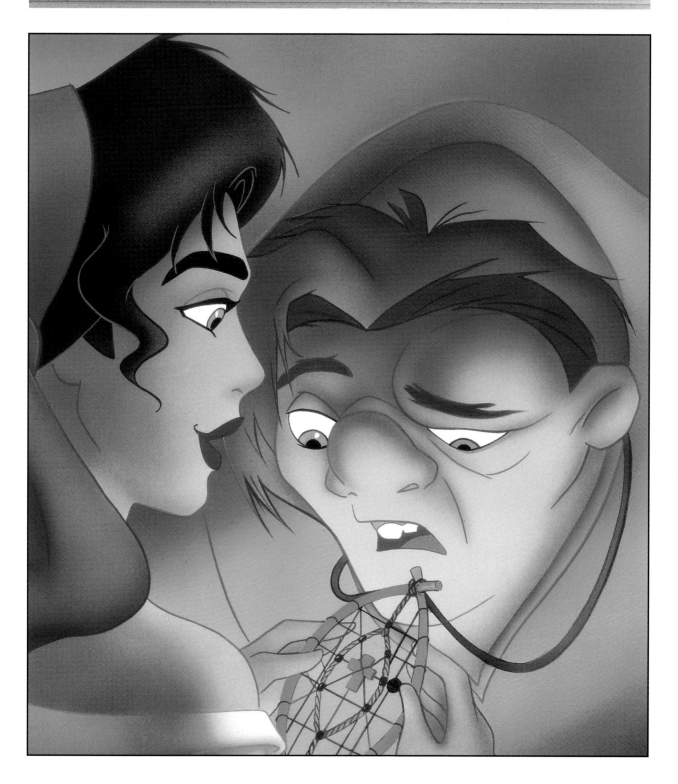

Esmeralda took off her necklace. "Here," she said. "Use this if *you* ever need a safe place. It will show you the way to our hideout, the Court of Miracles."

The thudding sound of heavy boots rounded the corner.

"Soldiers!" whispered Quasimodo. "Hurry, you've got to go." He helped Esmeralda to climb down to the ground. Then he handed Djali to her.

He waited until they were out of sight. Then, smiling to himself, Quasimodo turned and began the long climb back up Notre Dame to the bell tower. When he reached the top, a hand reached down and pulled him onto the parapet.

It was Phoebus. "I'm looking for the gypsy girl," he said. "Have you seen her?"

Quasimodo was so furious he could hardly speak. He lunged at Phoebus. "Get out!" he shouted, angrily. He pulled a flaming torch from the wall and began to swing it at Phoebus. "No soldiers! Sanctuary!"

Startled, Phoebus backed down the steps. "Wait," he said. "I mean her no harm. All I want is to…"

Quasimodo wouldn't listen. "*Go!*" He swung the burning torch wildly in front of him. Phoebus drew his sword and trapped the torch against the wall as he desperately tried to get Quasimodo to listen to him.

"You must give her a message from me," Phoebus said. "Tell her I didn't mean to trap her here. But it was the only way I could save her life. Will you tell her that?"

"I will if you go *now*," Quasimodo answered.

"All right," said Phoebus. He turned to leave, then stopped. "One more thing," he said. "Tell Esmeralda she's very lucky—lucky to have a friend like you."

"Just go," said Quasimodo. Then he thought for a moment about what Phoebus had said. A smile lit up his face. He proudly puffed out his chest and marched into the bell tower.

The gargoyles greeted him with shouts of congratulations.

"Well done!" Victor proclaimed. "You ejected that tin-plated buffoon with great panache."

"The nerve of him, snoopin' around here, tryin' to steal your girl," said Hugo.

Quasimodo's mouth dropped open. "*My* girl?"

"You remember—dark hair, works with a goat," Laverne reminded him.

"Way to go, lover boy!" exclaimed Hugo.

"L-l-lover boy!" stammered Quasimodo. "Not me."

"Don't be so modest," said Laverne.

"Look, it's nice of you to want to help," Quasimodo told his friends, "but I have 'the ugliest face in all of Paris'—remember?" He walked away. "I have to ring the bells for vespers."

*   *   *

From the dark, chilly tower, the bells called the people to evening prayer. As Quasimodo pulled the ropes, the events of the past hours drifted through his head.

58

He gazed out at the dark, flowing river. Two lovers walked hand in hand along its bank. He'd seen the same sight so many times. But he'd never dreamt for a moment that he could share the happiness of love. Now, as if from heaven, Esmeralda – one who didn't see his ugliness – had come into his life.

"Is it possible," he asked himself, "that she might *really* care for someone like me?"

Quasimodo went inside and picked up a piece of wood and his knife. Carefully he carved a little figure. It was of Esmeralda. He placed her in his miniature town, next to the model of himself – in the centre of the open square.

*   *   *

At midnight, a light was still shining in the Palace of Justice. Frollo, his head bowed, knelt in prayer.

"Help me," he pleaded. "You know I am so much better than these people. But the gypsy, Esmeralda, is tempting me. Guilt and shame should not be mine, for I am a righteous man. Please, I beg of you, do not let me fall under her spell."

In anguish, Frollo fell silent, struggling to find an answer. *Maybe it is God's will*, he thought at last, *for me to show her the way of righteousness.*

Raising his head, he spoke aloud, "And if she will not be mine and mine alone, she must face the fires of damnation!"

There was a knock at the door.

"Minister Frollo, the gypsy has escaped," a guard informed him.

"What?" Frollo didn't want to believe it. "How?"

"She's nowhere in the cathedral, Sir," the guard said. "She's gone."

Frollo stormed around his chamber, pounding his fist into his hand. "I'll find her! I'll find her if I have to burn down all of Paris!"

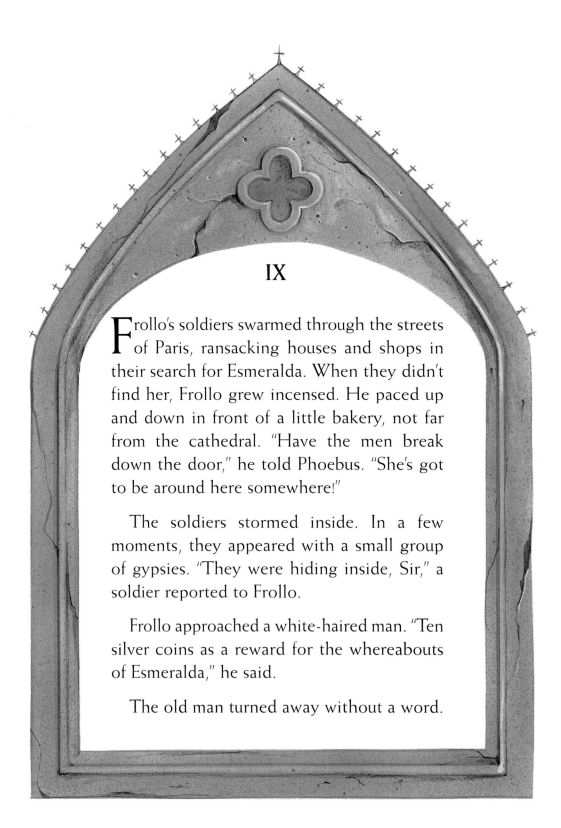

IX

Frollo's soldiers swarmed through the streets of Paris, ransacking houses and shops in their search for Esmeralda. When they didn't find her, Frollo grew incensed. He paced up and down in front of a little bakery, not far from the cathedral. "Have the men break down the door," he told Phoebus. "She's got to be around here somewhere!"

The soldiers stormed inside. In a few moments, they appeared with a small group of gypsies. "They were hiding inside, Sir," a soldier reported to Frollo.

Frollo approached a white-haired man. "Ten silver coins as a reward for the whereabouts of Esmeralda," he said.

The old man turned away without a word.

"Anyone else?" asked Frollo. "I'm sure you can't resist the money."

He received no response. "Lock them up!" ordered Frollo.

"Sir," Phoebus enquired, "is it worth all this merely to capture the gypsy girl?"

Frollo glared. "Are you questioning my judgment?"

"No, Your Honour, but I am uneasy with it…" Phoebus began.

A soldier galloped up on horseback. "A gypsy talisman has been found on the miller's property," he informed Frollo.

Frollo smiled. "Well then," he said, "we must pay the miller a little visit."

*　　*　　*

The miller answered the knock on his door. His wife stood behind him, holding a baby in her arms. Another child peeped out from behind her dress.

"Good day, Minister Frollo," he said. "What brings you…?"

Frollo pushed him back and burst inside. "Have you been harbouring gypsies?" he demanded.

"My wife and I always open our door to any weary traveller," said the miller. "Have mercy, my lord."

"I'm placing you and your family under house arrest until I get to the bottom of this," Frollo told him. "If what you say is true, and you are innocent, you have nothing to fear."

"You will find that I am innocent," the miller said.

Frollo left the mill and shut the door. He mounted his horse, took a flaming torch from one of his soldiers, and handed it down to Phoebus. "Burn the mill!"

Phoebus was shocked. "With all due respect, Sir, I wasn't trained to harm the innocent."

"But you *were* trained to follow orders," Frollo said.

Phoebus looked Frollo straight in the eye. "Not the orders of a madman," he declared, extinguishing the torch in a barrel of water.

"Insolent coward!" barked Frollo. "I'll do it myself!" Frollo grabbed another torch from one of his men and set fire to the mill. The flames quickly spread to the thatched roof.

Phoebus leapt through a window into the smoke-filled mill. In a short time, he emerged with the miller's children in his arms. The miller and his wife stumbled out behind him.

"Captain Phoebus," Frollo cried out, "you will be punished for this insolence!" He motioned to his soldiers. "Seize him!"

Not far away, peering cautiously from the folds of her cloak, Esmerialda watched in horror. Hurriedly she searched about for a stone. Then, taking careful aim, she threw it.

The stone shot towards Frollo and struck his horse squarely on the rump. The startled animal reared and Frollo was thrown to the ground.

Before the confused soldiers could react, Phoebus leapt onto Frollo's horse and galloped towards the river.

"Shoot him!" cried Frollo. "Don't let him escape!"

The soldiers rode hard after Phoebus. Just as he reached the bridge over the river, an arrow struck him in the shoulder. Phoebus lost his grip on the reins, and fell from the horse's back into the water.

Frollo trotted up and studied the river closely. All he could see were air bubbles. "Well done," he said to his men. "Now, get back to town. You must find the gypsy, even if you have to burn every building to the ground!"

Concealed at the base of the bridge, Esmeralda watched them go. Then she slipped into the water. She surfaced with Phoebus in her grasp and, with strong strokes, swam for shore.

*   *   *

At nightfall, Frollo, riding his stallion, surveyed the blazing streets of Paris.

A sergeant rode up to him. "We've looked everywhere," he reported. "There's still no sign of the gypsy. Shall I call off the search now?"

For a few moments, Frollo sat still and studied Notre Dame, silhouetted against the fiery sky. He was puzzled. How in the world had she escaped from the cathedral with a guard posted at every door? As he raised his eyes to the cathedral bell tower, it suddenly came to him – Quasimodo had defied him! He'd helped that wretched gypsy elude her fate. As the shock of his initial anger subsided, a sly smile crossed Frollo's face. "Not just yet," the wily minister told the sergeant, "I still have one more card to play..."

*   *   *

Quasimodo watched in alarm from the bell tower. "The whole city's burning down!" he cried.

"Quasi, pay attention," said Victor. "It's your turn."

Quasimodo waved his arms towards the window. "How can you play cards at a time like this? Just look out there!"

"Don't worry," said Hugo. "Cathedrals are fireproof."

"I'm not worried about us," said Quasimodo. "I'm worried about Esmeralda."

"From what I've seen, Esmeralda can take care of herself," said Laverne.

Quasimodo looked out over the glowing city. "I don't know... this is really dangerous."

"When things cool off," Laverne assured him, "she'll be back."

"What makes you so sure?" Quasimodo asked.

"She likes you," said Laverne.

"Do you think so?" asked Quasimodo, looking doubtful.

"Sure," said Hugo. "You're a swell guy – one of a kind. And another thing... wait a second..." He suddenly cupped his hand to his ear. "Somebody's comin'!"

"Quasimodo? Are you there?" called a voice.

"It's Esmeralda!" cried Quasimodo. He ran to the door.

Esmeralda's hair hung in damp strings around her face. Her soiled cloak clung to her.

"What happened?" gasped Quasimodo. "Are you all right?"

Esmeralda took his hand in hers. "I'm fine," she said. "I was lucky. One of the guards fell asleep and I sneaked past him. But I have to ask for your help again."

"Anything," he told her.

Esmeralda glanced towards the steps. In a moment, two gypsy men carried Phoebus, unconscious, into the room. Djali trotted behind.

"He was shot by one of Frollo's men," Esmeralda explained. Her eyes grew tearful. "Will you keep him here?"

Quasimodo nodded and the men placed Phoebus on the bed.

Phoebus' eyes fluttered open. "Esmeralda…"

She put her finger lightly on his lips. "*Shhh*. You can hide here until you're strong enough to move."

Quasimodo brought a bowl of water and a clean cloth.

"Fortune must have been with you, Phoebus," Esmeralda said, cleaning his wound. "That arrow almost pierced your heart."

Phoebus smiled weakly and kissed her hand. "I'm not so sure it didn't." Esmeralda leaned over and kissed him back.

Quasimodo felt his own heart break. Stifling a sob, he turned away.

Suddenly, Djali bleated an alarm. Quasimodo rushed to look out of the window. "Frollo's coming!" he cried. "Hurry – go down the south tower steps."

"Be careful, my brave friend," Esmeralda told Quasimodo. "Promise me you won't let anything happen to him."

Quasimodo nodded. "I promise."

She patted his cheek. "Thank you." Then she was gone.

As fast as he was able, Quasimodo lifted Phoebus from the bed, hid him under a table and covered it with a tablecloth.

Moments later, Frollo entered the bell tower. He was carrying a little covered basket.

"Master," said Quasimodo, trying to keep his voice steady. "I didn't think you would be coming."

Frollo sat at the table and looked expectantly at Quasimodo. "Well?" he asked.

"Oh, sorry," said Quasimodo. He scurried about and set the table.

"Grapes for you, dear boy," Frollo said at last, opening the basket. "I'm never too busy to share a meal with you."

A grape rolled across the table and tumbled onto the floor. Quasimodo sprang from his seat and picked it up. He blinked hard – Phoebus' hand was sticking out from under the cloth. Quickly, he pushed it back.

"You seem a bit nervous," said Frollo. "Is something troubling you? Are you hiding something from me?"

"Me? Oh *no*, Master." Quasimodo sat back at the table.

"You're not eating," said Frollo.

Quasimodo shoved a handful of grapes into his mouth.

"*Mmmm*. These are very good," he said. "*Mmmm*."

Phoebus let out a little moan.

"*Mmmmmm*," repeated Quasimodo. "Very good indeed."

Frollo rose from the table. "What's... *different* in here?" he asked, looking around the bell tower.

"Nothing, Sir," answered Quasimodo, almost frozen with fright.

Frollo glanced at the miniature town. Then he picked up the figure of Esmeralda. "Isn't this one new?" he asked. "It looks very much like the gypsy girl."

His eyes narrowing with hatred, Frollo put his face very close to Quasimodo's. "I *know*," he said. "I know you helped her to escape."

Quasimodo gulped and cowered away from his master.

"And now all of Paris is burning!" Frollo's face trembled with rage. "All because of *you!*"

"Sh-sh-she was kind to me, Master," said Quasimodo.

"You idiot!" roared Frollo. He looked at Quasimodo's miniature town. Then, with a sweep of his arm, he knocked it onto the floor. "She has you under her spell! Haven't I told you time and again that gypsies aren't capable of real love? You of all people should know that – think of your own mother!"

Then all at once Frollo's furious outburst was over, and he became strangely calm. He put his arm around Quasimodo's shoulder. "Well," he said softly, "I will soon free you from Esmeralda's evil spell."

"What do you mean?" asked Quasimodo.

Frollo spoke slowly and clearly. "Listen *carefully* to me," he said. "I've discovered where her hideout is. Tomorrow at dawn, I will attack with a thousand men."

Snatching up the figure of Esmeralda, Frollo took his knife and plunged it into the little wooden model. Then he set the model on fire, tossed it to the floor, and left the room.

As Quasimodo, numb with shock, stared at the charred figurine, Phoebus crawled out from under the table. Groggily he struggled to his feet.

"We must find the Court of Miracles before dawn," he said, getting ready to leave. "We've got to warn them!" He stopped at the door and looked back at Quasimodo, questioningly. "Well?" he said. "Are you coming with me?"

Quasimodo shook his head. "I can't."

Phoebus raised his eyebrows in surprise. "I thought you were Esmeralda's friend."

"I am," said Quasimodo. "But Frollo is my master. I can't disobey him again."

"Esmeralda stood up for you," said Phoebus. "You've got a funny way of showing gratitude."

Quasimodo winced at his words. Should he help Phoebus find Esmeralda and warn her of Frollo's plans to attack her people? He knew Phoebus spoke the truth but he was also afraid of disobeying Frollo again.

"Well, I'm not going to sit back and watch Frollo continue with his evil deeds," Phoebus declared. Holding his wounded shoulder, he staggered from the room.

Quasimodo stood there quietly. He took Esmeralda's necklace from inside his shirt and gazed at it. Frollo was right—Esmeralda didn't love him after all. If she loved anyone, it was Phoebus. So why should he

put himself in danger to help her? And how could he take another chance on a world where people had treated him so cruelly?

Still… Esmeralda had rescued him at the festival, while Frollo had calmly watched and done nothing. But Frollo was his master. Yet Esmeralda, at a time when she hardly knew him, had risked her own safety for his…

In his heart, Quasimodo knew there was only one answer. He knew what he must do. Without wasting another moment, he rushed to join Phoebus.

X

Phoebus cautiously opened one of the side doors. He peeped out and breathed a sigh of relief. Not a soldier in sight. If he could make it across the square unseen, he'd be on his way. From out of nowhere, Quasimodo appeared hanging upside down from a ledge. He did a somersault and landed in front of Phoebus. "Good grief, man," Phoebus cried out. "You startled me!"

"*Shhh,*" whispered Quasimodo. "I'm coming with you."

"Glad you changed your mind," said Phoebus.

"I'm doing it for her—not for you," Quasimodo told him. He showed Phoebus Esmeralda's necklace. "She said this would help us find her."

Phoebus studied it. "It's got some sort of charm or talisman hanging from it. It must be a code."

"I think it's a map," said Quasimodo. "You see," he pointed with his finger, "the cross represents the cathedral. And the lines are the streets of the city."

"A map?" scoffed Phoebus. "I've been in battles on four continents and I think I've got a pretty good idea what a map looks like—and this is not it."

"Well," said Quasimodo, "I've lived up in the bell tower for twenty years and I think I know what this city looks like from above. And this *is* it!"

"Fine," said Phoebus at last. "If you say it's a map, it's a map. But look, if we're going to help Esmeralda, we'd better call a truce."

"All right," agreed Quasimodo. He pointed to the talisman again. "Look at this pointed symbol. It's placed inside the city graveyard—I'll bet that's the Court of Miracles. I know just where it is," Quasimodo told him. "I've seen it from the bell tower."

As soon as they crossed the square and disappeared into a side alley, a figure stepped out of the shadows of Notre Dame. It was Frollo. He'd been listening to their every word!

Keeping a safe distance behind Quasimodo and Phoebus, Frollo led his troops through the moonlit city. At the edge of town, he saw them go up to the cemetery gate.

* * *

As Quasimodo pushed open the heavy iron gate, its rusted hinges creaked. He helped to steady Phoebus, who was weak from the long

walk. Nervously they entered the quiet graveyard. The headstones, standing like ghostly sentinels, gleamed in the moonlight.

An owl, disturbed by the men's approach, swooped past on silent wings. Startled, Quasimodo and Phoebus ducked.

Then, cautiously, they began to search the graveyard. Several minutes later, Quasimodo nudged Phoebus. A large pointed tomb loomed before them.

"This looks like the symbol on the map!" exclaimed Phoebus.

Quasimodo fingered the cold marble surface and felt a deep groove. He traced its outline. "Phoebus!" he cried, removing the cover. Right inside the entrance, a torch flickered in an iron holder. It lit the way down a flight of steps.

"It leads underground," breathed Phoebus. "I'm glad you decided to come along, Quasimodo. A little trip through the dark, rat-infested catacombs is always more fun when you bring a friend!"

At the bottom of the steps, a torchlit room opened up before them. The room was lined with skeletons sitting propped against the walls.

"This doesn't seem right to me," Phoebus said. "We should have run into something by now. A guard, or a booby trap, or..."

Suddenly, some of the skeletons leaning against the walls sprang to their feet. In the blink of an eye, Phoebus and Quasimodo were surrounded.

"They're not skeletons at all," said Quasimodo in shock. "They're men wearing disguises!"

One man stepped forward. Quasimodo recognised him at once. It was Clopin, the man he'd seen at the festival.

"Well, well, well," the leader of the gypsies began. "What have we here?"

"Trespassers! Spies!" shouted two of his men.

"We're not spies. Listen to us," Phoebus protested. "You've got to listen!"

Clopin turned to his men. "Bind and gag them!"

From all sides, the angry men closed in. They bound Quasimodo and Phoebus and carried them into a large chamber.

Clopin gestured to the room. "So, now you have seen the Court of Miracles. How very clever of you to have found our hideout. Unfortunately, you won't live to tell the tale."

Quasimodo and Phoebus were desperate to tell Esmeralda that Frollo was preparing to attack the gypsies but they could not see her anywhere. Then suddenly, Esmeralda ran into the court and pushed her way towards Clopin. "Stop! These men are our friends!" she told him.

Clopin was amazed. "They are?"

"This soldier saved the miller's family," explained Esmeralda, "and Quasimodo helped me escape from the cathedral."

Phoebus faced the crowd. "We came to warn you – Frollo's coming!"

"He told me he knows where you are hiding," added Quasimodo, "and he's attacking at dawn with a thousand men."

The crowd stirred in fear.

"We can't waste any time," Esmeralda said to her people. "If Frollo intends to attack at dawn, we must leave by midnight!"

She turned to Phoebus. "You took a terrible risk coming here. It may not exactly show, but we're very grateful."

"Don't thank me," said Phoebus, "thank Quasimodo. He's the real hero."

Esmeralda hugged Quasimodo. "I think I know that better than anyone," she said.

"Without this man's help," said Phoebus, addressing the gypsies, "I never would have found my way here."

"Nor would I!" boomed a voice. Frollo stood triumphant at the entrance. His soldiers blocked all means of escape.

The Minister of Justice walked to the centre of the room. "After twenty years of searching, the Court of Miracles is mine at last. As the proverb goes... Good things come to those who wait... listen... and *follow*!"

He smiled at Quasimodo and ruffled his hair. "Dear boy, I always knew one day you'd be of use to me," he said. "You led me right here."

Quasimodo's eyes grew wide. "Oh no..." He buried his face in his hands.

Esmeralda flew to Quasimodo's defence. "You tricked him!" she told Frollo.

Frollo ignored her. "And look what else I've caught in my net. It's Captain Phoebus, back from his watery grave. I shall remedy that," he said.

"And as for you," Frollo continued, sneering at Esmeralda, "you too shall pay for disobeying me!" Frollo motioned to his sergeant. "Lock them up."

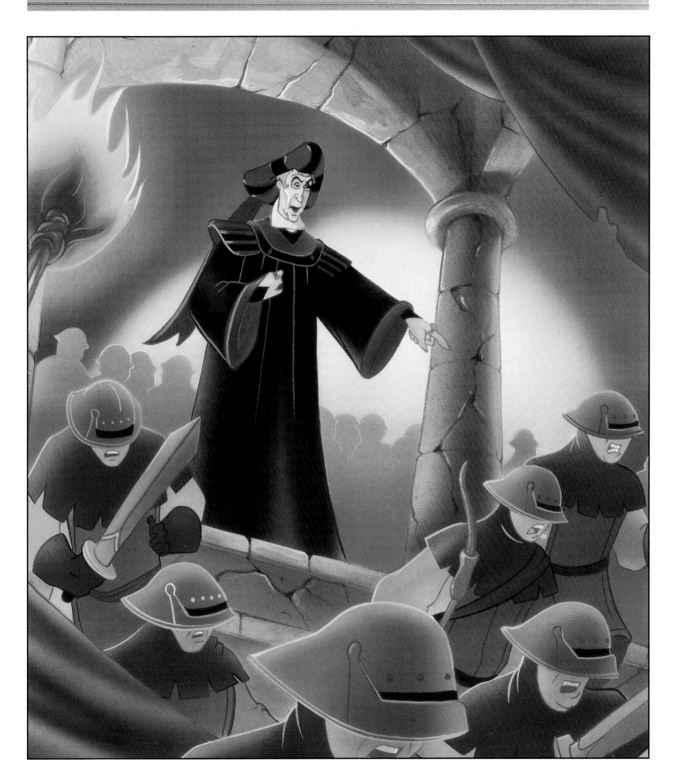

Quasimodo clutched at Frollo's cape. "No, please…"

Frollo brushed him away. "Take this one back to the bell tower. And make certain he can't escape."

The soldiers took the prisoners away, and Quasimodo, overcome with grief, collapsed on the floor.

XI

The next day at sunset, a crowd gathered in the square. Caged prison carts carrying the gypsies and Phoebus rolled to the foot of Notre Dame. In the centre of the square, Esmeralda stood tied to a wooden post.

Frollo climbed onto a high platform in the centre of the square. "The prisoner, Esmeralda," he announced, "has been found guilty. The sentence," he boomed, "is *death!*"

Powerless to help, the Archdeacon looked on sadly from the cathedral door. Frollo's men had surrounded him.

The crowd pushed forward towards the platform. "Release her!" cried a townswoman. "She's done nothing wrong."

Frollo sneered at the angry crowd. He snapped his fingers and a soldier advanced with a flaming torch. Taking it, Frollo crossed the square to Esmeralda. "The time has come, gypsy," he said. "You stand on the brink of the abyss, yet even now it is not too late. I can save you from the flames of this world and the next if you choose to obey me!"

Esmeralda said nothing.

Frollo began to tremble. Esmeralda's defiant silence spoke more than a thousand words. Enraged, he faced the crowd. "The gypsy has made her decision. She leaves me with no choice..."

* * *

In the bell tower, a chained Quasimodo knelt between two columns of stone. His head hung down as he stared hopelessly at the floor.

"C'mon, Quasi, snap out of it," pleaded Hugo. "You've gotta break these chains! You can do it—you're the strongest guy in town!"

"It's all my fault," mumbled Quasimodo, despondently.

"You *cannot* let Frollo win," Victor insisted.

"He already has," Quasimodo said, sighing.

"So that's it?" asked Hugo. "You're giving up?"

"You know," Laverne told Quasimodo, "these chains aren't what's holding you back. I think you're still jealous."

"*Leave me alone!*" Quasimodo snapped at them.

"Okay, Quasimodo," said Hugo, with a sob in his voice. "We'll leave you alone."

"After all," Victor added, "we're only made of stone." He looked away, deeply hurt.

Laverne shook her head, sadly. "We just thought *you* were made of something stronger."

The gargoyles turned to stone.

Quasimodo listened as Frollo's booming voice addressed the crowd below.

"She stands before you," Frollo cried, "exposed for the monster that she is. Therefore, it is my duty to see that she no longer lives on earth!"

The crowd roared as one. *"Noooo!"*

"Noooo!" Quasimodo roared, too. He strained against the heavy chains. They held fast. Using every bit of his strength, he pulled again. Little cracks zig-zagged down the columns.

As Quasimodo struggled, a column toppled over and shook the bell tower. The bells of Notre Dame swayed and began to toll. In a few minutes he managed to tug the chains loose.

Free at last, Quasimodo grabbed a long rope and tore to the edge of the parapet. Tying one end of the rope around a pillar, he flung his legs over the side and lowered himself from ledge to ledge.

Meanwhile, Frollo threw a torch onto the dry straw and stood back as it caught fire. Overcome by the heat of the flames and the stifling smoke, Esmeralda fell unconscious.

Suddenly, before the astonished crowd, Quasimodo swung into the square. He beat back some soldiers caught off guard. Then he pushed Frollo aside, untied Esmeralda and swept her away.

"Quasimodo!" everyone shouted, cheering him on.

A few moments later, Quasimodo reappeared on the cathedral balcony. Holding Esmeralda above his head, he cried, "Sanctuary! Sanctuary! Sanctuary!"

"Sanctuary!" the crowd returned his cry. "Sanctuary!"

Quasimodo disappeared into the cathedral with Esmeralda. Gently he placed her, still unconscious, on a pallet in his workroom.

Down below, a livid Frollo fumed. "Seize the cathedral!" he screamed to his men.

Quasimodo climbed onto a parapet with a wooden beam in his arms. He heaved it to the street below, where it crashed into Frollo's carriage, sending splinters and chunks of wood everywhere.

Several soldiers fled.

"Come back, you cowards!" shouted Frollo.

A line of soldiers hoisted the heavy beam to their shoulders. Running with it, they rammed it against the cathedral door.

Taking advantage of the confusion, Phoebus freed himself and Clopin. He leapt on top of the prison cart and shouted to the crowd, "Citizens of Paris! Frollo has persecuted our people, ransacked our city... and now he has declared war on Notre Dame herself. Will we allow it?"

"*Noooo!*" cried the crowd.

Phoebus and Clopin freed the caged gypsies. Snatching a sword from one of the soldiers, Phoebus forged a path to the cathedral. But Frollo's army continued its assault on it. Swarming like bees, the

soldiers climbed the walls, while in the square below they battered at the doors.

Quasimodo was exhausted. "It's hopeless," he said, looking down from the bell tower. "I can't fight them all off." He covered his ears to keep out the clanging of the bells.

"Listen," said Victor. "I detect a sour note – one of the bells may have a crack in it."

"That's it!" said Quasimodo. He jumped to his feet.

"What's it?" Hugo asked, chasing after him.

"If a bell has a crack, it's repaired with molten lead, right?" asked Quasimodo.

"Right!" said Hugo. "Very hot stuff!"

"Well," Quasimodo said, "some of that *very hot stuff* is heating up in the vat room."

"*Ahhh!*" said Hugo, Laverne and Victor. "Let's get going!"

The vat, filled with molten lead, stood in the corner of the room. Using all their might, the gargoyles struggled to tip it over.

"This... is... one... time..." panted Hugo, "when it's good to have hands of stone!"

"Right!" joked Laverne. "They really come in hand-y!"

At last, with Quasimodo pushing a beam hard against the vat, they tipped it over. The glowing liquid flowed towards the balcony and cascaded down to the street.

Below, in the square, Frollo frantically sprinted back and forth shouting orders. "Batter down the doors!"

The huge doors stood firm. *"Again!"* roared Frollo.

Without warning, a shower of red-hot lead rained down from the sky. At once, the shouting soldiers dropped the beam and fled in terror. The men scaling the walls scrambled down as fast as they could.

"Cowards!" yelled Frollo. He waited for a break in the fiery cascade. Then he rushed forward and inspected the door. There were several breaks in the wood. He pried open a small gap with his sword and just managed to squeeze through.

* * *

Quasimodo leaned out and looked at the deserted square. "We've done it!" he cried. "We've beaten them back."

He tore into his room. "Come and see! Esmeralda, wake up!" he said, rubbing her hand. It fell back limp on the bed.

"Oh no," gasped Quasimodo.

Then, from the corner of his eye, he caught sight of a moving shadow. It was Frollo, holding a raised dagger.

Quasimodo jumped to his feet. Effortlessly, he wrenched the dagger away and threw it aside.

Frollo, thrown off balance, fell to the floor. "Now, now… listen to me!" he said.

"No, Frollo, *you* listen," Quasimodo told him. "All my life you've told me that the world's a cruel place. But now I see that the only thing that's dark and cruel about it is *you!*"

Esmeralda stirred. "Quasimodo?" she asked.

Quasimodo picked Esmeralda up in his arms and ran from the room. Frollo scrambled to his feet and charged after them.

Quasimodo made his way out along the parapet. He reached for a ledge and hoisted himself onto it, then grabbed hold of Esmeralda and helped her up. Inching along the narrow ledge, they managed to turn the corner.

"Leaving so soon?" asked Frollo, standing before them with his sword drawn. "You've been a thorn in my side long enough, Quasimodo. Now I'm going to do what I should have done twenty years ago!"

He leapt onto a gargoyle that jutted over the square. In a whirl of black velvet, he whipped off his cape and flung it at Quasimodo. Caught by surprise, Quasimodo lost his footing and stumbled. As he slipped from the ledge, Esmeralda grabbed his hand and held him. Quasimodo hung in midair.

Frollo laughed in triumph and swung his sword high. Esmeralda screamed. She was losing her grip on Quasimodo. At any moment, he would fall.

But then Frollo heard the crack of stone. The gargoyle was breaking beneath him. As it snapped free, Frollo, screaming, plunged to the square far below.

Though she was using all the strength she could summon, Esmeralda couldn't hold on to Quasimodo any longer. Slowly he slipped from her fingers.

"Quasimodo! No!" she cried out.

But at the moment he fell, two strong arms suddenly reached out from a window just below and grabbed him. Swiftly, they pulled him inside to safety.

Esmeralda looked down and saw Phoebus smiling back.

Phoebus laughed. "Nothing like being in the right place at the right time," he said, patting Quasimodo on the shoulder. "I looked out and there were your legs – dangling in the air!"

Then his voice grew soft. "I'm glad that I didn't arrive a moment later."

In relief, the two friends embraced.

Esmeralda burst into the room and threw her arms around Quasimodo. He smiled at her and at Phoebus. Then he took each of his friends by the wrist and joined their hands together.

*   *   *

As the new day dawned, a crowd gathered in front of the cathedral, eager to celebrate the victory over Frollo and his cruelty. As soon as Phoebus and Esmeralda appeared in the doorway, they were greeted with smiles and cheers from the grateful townspeople.

But Quasimodo hung back. He wasn't sure if he could face the world again after all that had happened. Smiling encouragingly, Esmeralda held out her hand to him. At last, blinking in the dawn's pale light, he hesitantly stepped outside.

As he stood on the cathedral steps, the crowd in the square fell silent. Everyone seemed uncertain of what to say or do.

Then a little girl came forward and tugged at Quasimodo's sleeve. Quasimodo bent down and she smiled at him, reaching up gently to touch his face. Taking his hand, she led him down the steps and into the crowd.

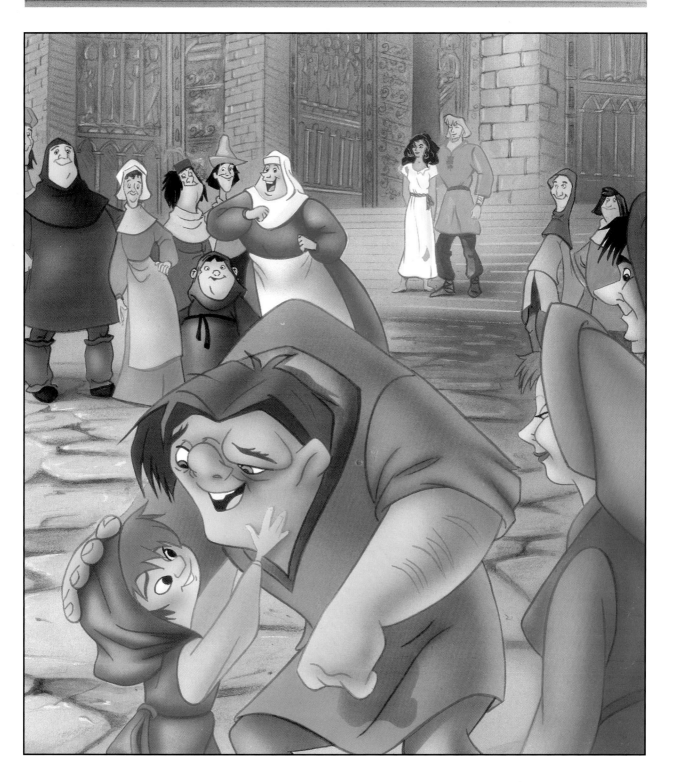

"Quasimodo! Quasimodo! Quasimodo!" everybody shouted. Quasimodo couldn't believe what was happening—he thought his heart would burst with happiness.

Clopin and some townsmen lifted him high on their shoulders and paraded triumphantly around the square. And that morning the city walls echoed with joyous cheers for Quasimodo—the hero of Notre Dame!